The T

T0247222

VISTA®
HIGHER LEARNING

Boston, Massachusetts

ELA

It's quarter to eight. It's the first day of classes. Alex sits down near a new girl with **glasses**.

She has lots of books. Maybe eight, nine, or ten. She writes in a notebook. She has a green pen.

a bright purple dress

Her dress is bright purple. She has big red hair.
She looks up. She **smiles** when she sees Alex there.

The girl says, "I'm writing a book. Look and see!
Let's meet after school at the big yellow tree."

hanging out at the mall

Then Alex has lunch with his close friend named Russ.
"That new girl is strange," Russ says. "She's not like us."

"Don't meet her," says Layla. "It will not look cool.
Come hang out with *us* at the mall after school!"

scooter

But Alex does go. Yes, he goes to the tree.
The girl is there waiting. As strange as can be!

Her name is Amanda. She's like a computer!
She's funny and smart. And she has a cool scooter!

The next day in class, students read on the board:
TEAM GAME NEXT FRIDAY! PLAY! WIN AN **AWARD**!

Amanda asks Alex, "Can I work with you?"
"Of course!" Alex says. "We're a good team of two."

He sees Russ, Mikayla, and Layla, and Jake.
They say, "Be on *our* team! Don't make a mistake!"

They say, "We're the *best* team. Do you want to lose?
You're *our* friend or *hers*, Alex. You need to choose!"

Alex stands still. He has nothing to say.
He picks up his backpack. Then, he walks away.

He sees a strange **bird** at his window that night.
It says to him, "What?" Then, it flies out of sight.

"What *what?*" Alex asks. He looks out at the yard.
"What should I do now? I don't know! That's so hard!"

The next day he looks for Amanda to say,
"I need to change teams. My friends need me to play."

Amanda is sad. He feels sorry. However,
his friends are his friends. Can he tell them "no"? Never!

The bird comes that night. Alex jumps out of bed.
Its eyes are deep black and its **feathers** are red.

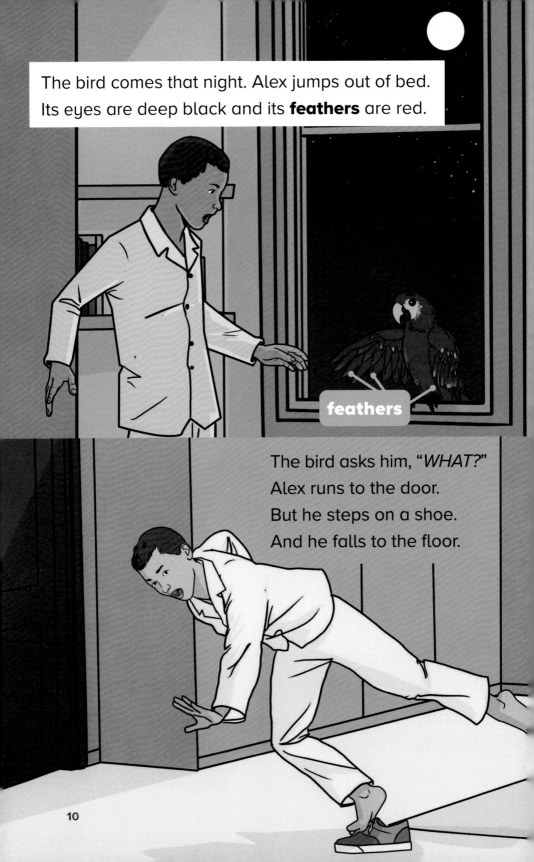

feathers

The bird asks him, "*WHAT?*"
Alex runs to the door.
But he steps on a shoe.
And he falls to the floor.

Then he sees something strange. It's a kind of a **dream**. He's with his four friends. They are on the same team.

They're losing the game. But his friends just don't care. They joke. They all laugh at Amanda's red hair!

Alex is thinking twice. He's thinking again about what to do.

Alex can see that his friends are not nice.
He liked them before. He is now thinking twice!

Morning comes soon. Alex wakes up in bed.
He thinks very hard about what the bird said.

He looks for Amanda. He waves. He calls,
"Hey!" He says he is sorry about yesterday.

They work as a team. The "Two A's" is their name.
Together they win the award in the game!

His old friends seem **angry**. They give him a stare.
The Two A's aren't looking. They really don't care.

"It's true," Alex thinks. "That Amanda *is* strange.
But that makes her fun! She does *not* need to change!"

The friends look at Alex for a long time. They stare at Alex.

angry

TEAM COOL

TEAM COOL

TEAM COOL

And the strange bird that visited Alex before?
It never comes back to ask, "What?" anymore.

Alex learned a big lesson that helps him a lot.
Now he knows "what" he should do and "what"
he should not!

glasses

smile

team

award

bird

feathers

dream

angry